Cultural Traditions in Poland

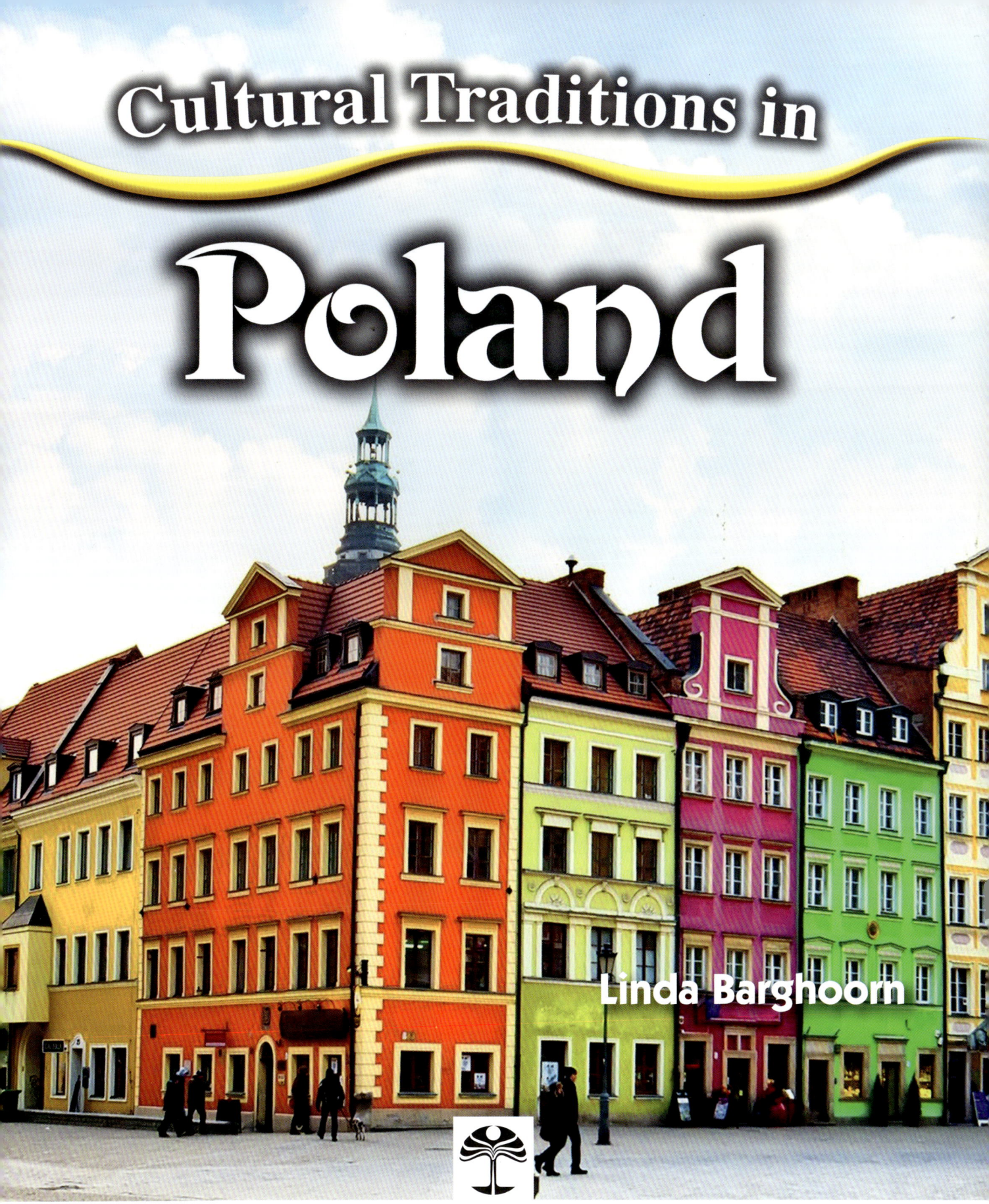

Linda Barghoorn

Crabtree Publishing Company
www.crabtreebooks.com

Crabtree Publishing Company
www.crabtreebooks.com

Author: Linda Barghoorn

Publishing plan research and development:
Reagan Miller

Editorial director: Kathy Middleton

Editor: Ellen Rodger

Proofreader: Wendy Scavuzzo

Photo research: Abigail Smith

Designer: Abigail Smith

Production coordinator and prepress technician:
Abigail Smith

Print coordinator: Margaret Amy Salter

Cover: Ruins of a medieval castle tower in Mirow, Poland (top and middle background); Folk dancers performing a dance in costume (middle); traditional hurdy-gurdy instrument (middle); painted miniature nativity scene (bottom left); oriental poppies (bottom right)

Title page: Colorful buildings in Wroclaw city center

Photographs:
Alamy: Paul Gapper, p11;
Library of Congress: Wolcott, Marion Post, p24 (inset)
Shutterstock: © Stanislaw Tokarski, front cover (dancers), p13 (bottom); © Florin Cnejevici, front cover (bottom middle); © De Visu, pp12, 13 (top); © Kapa1966, p14; © Tomasz Bidermann, p15; © Michal Ludwiczak, p18; © Michal Ludwiczak, p19 (bkgd); © Dziurek, p24–25 (bkgd); © Agnes Kantaruk, front cover (botton left), p28; © Yuliia Fesyk, p29; © praszkiewicz, p31
Wikimedia Commons: Ratomir Wilkowski, p8; T. Kicin, p9

All other images by Shutterstock

Library and Archives Canada Cataloguing in Publication

Barghoorn, Linda, author
    Cultural traditions in Poland / Linda Barghoorn.

(Cultural traditions in my world)
Includes index.
Issued in print and electronic formats.
ISBN 978-0-7787-8098-4 (hardcover).--
ISBN 978-0-7787-8106-6 (softcover).--
ISBN 978-1-4271-1953-7 (HTML)

    1. Holidays--Poland--Juvenile literature. 2. Festivals--Poland--Juvenile literature. 3. Poland--Social life and customs--Juvenile literature. I. Title. II. Series: Cultural traditions in my world

GT4871.P6B37 2017   j394.269438   C2017-903528-2
    C2017-903529-0

Library of Congress Cataloging-in-Publication Data

Names: Barghoorn, Linda, author.
Title: Cultural traditions in Poland / Linda Barghoorn.
Description: New York, New York : Crabtree Publishing, 2018.
Series: Cultural traditions in my world | Includes index. | Audience: Age 5-8. | Audience: Grade K to 3.
Identifiers: LCCN 2017024407 (print) | LCCN 2017027894 (ebook) | ISBN 9781427119537 (Electronic HTML) | ISBN 9780778780984 (reinforced library binding) | ISBN 9780778781066 (pbk.)
Subjects: LCSH: Festivals--Poland--Juvenile literature. | Poland--Social life and customs--Juvenile literature.
Classification: LCC GT4871.P6 (ebook) | LCC GT4871.P6 B37 2018 (print) | DDC 394.269438--dc23
LC record available at https://lccn.loc.gov/2017024407

Crabtree Publishing Company
www.crabtreebooks.com   1-800-387-7650

Printed in Canada/082017/EF20170629

Copyright © **2018 CRABTREE PUBLISHING COMPANY**. All rights reserved. No part of this publication may be reproduced, stored in a retrieval system or be transmitted in any form or by any means, electronic, mechanical, photocopying, recording, or otherwise, without the prior written permission of Crabtree Publishing Company. In Canada: We acknowledge the financial support of the Government of Canada through the Canada Book Fund for our publishing activities.

Published in Canada
Crabtree Publishing
616 Welland Ave.
St. Catharines, ON
L2M 5V6

Published in the United States
Crabtree Publishing
PMB 59051
350 Fifth Avenue, 59th Floor
New York, New York 10118

Published in the United Kingdom
Crabtree Publishing
Maritime House
Basin Road North, Hove
BN41 1WR

Published in Australia
Crabtree Publishing
3 Charles Street
Coburg North
VIC 3058

Contents

Welcome to Poland 4
Name Day and Weddings 6
The Drowning of Marzanna 8
Easter 10
Constitution Day
 and Independence Day 12
Corpus Christi 14
St. John's Eve 16
Harvest Festival 18
All Saints' Day 20
St. Andrew's Day 22
St. Barbara's Day 24
Christmas Eve 26
Christmas Day 28
New Year's Celebrations 30
Glossary and Index 32

Welcome to Poland

Poland is a country in northern Europe. More than 38 million people live there. Most people, about 85 percent of the population, are **Roman Catholic**. The Catholic religion plays an important part in Polish life. Many of Poland's traditions are based on the religion.

Poland's capital city has changed names three times, from Gniezno to Krakow to Warsaw. Today, Warsaw (below) is Poland's largest city, with 1.7 million people.

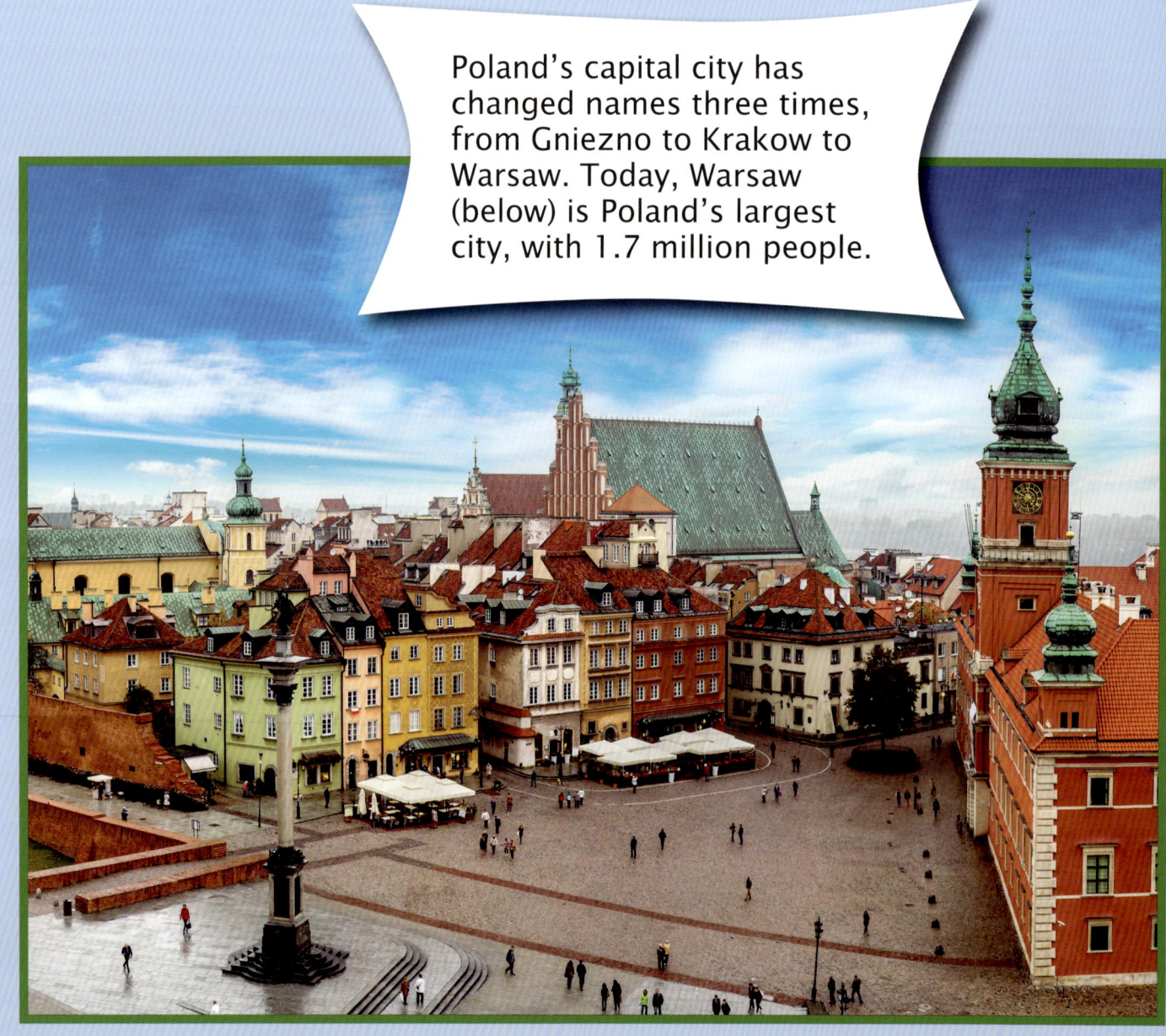

Cultural traditions are the beliefs, ceremonies, holidays, and customs that people celebrate in their country. Some cultural traditions celebrate events in peoples' lives, such as birthdays and weddings. Some honor important dates in the country's history. Others celebrate a religious event or folk tradition. This book highlights the many interesting cultural traditions of Poland.

Did You Know?
Most people in Poland speak Polish, which is a **Slavic** language.

Name Day and Weddings

Many Polish people are named after Roman Catholic **saints**. Each day of the Polish calendar honors a different saint. A person's Name Day is the day the saint they are named after is honored. Family and friends meet to share gifts and a meal. Name Days are more important than birthdays in Poland!

Did You Know?
The traditional song to celebrate a birthday is called Sto Lat, meaning "May You Live a Hundred Years."

When you celebrate someone's Name Day, you should wish them Wszytkiego Najlepszego, or "All the best!"

6

Weddings are lively and happy celebrations. After the wedding ceremony, guests throw coins at the bride and groom. They must pick up all the coins, which will bring them good luck. Later, the bride's and groom's parents give everyone a piece of salted bread, shown below, to eat. The bread represents wishes for good fortune. The salt reminds them of the challenges life may bring.

Although people wear modern clothing, traditional costumes are still worn on special occasions such as weddings.

The Drowning of Marzanna

The Drowning of Marzanna is an ancient tradition that is celebrated around the first day of spring or March 21. Marzanna is the Polish name for the Slavic goddess connected with nature, winter, and death. Her day is sometimes called Death Sunday.

These children stand with a Marzanna doll.

Each spring, villagers create a life-size doll made of straw and decorated with colorful ribbons. They take it to a nearby river where they set it on fire and throw it into the water to drown. This represents the wish for winter to end and for spring to begin.

Did You Know?
One **superstition** says that you should not touch the Marzanna doll once she is in the water, or your hand could shrink.

The Drowning of Marzanna is an ancient tradition, which means it began many years ago. This picture of the tradition is from the early 1900s.

Easter

Easter celebrations in Poland take place over many days. On Holy Saturday, families carry baskets of food to church to be blessed by the **priest**. These baskets are filled with bread, cakes, eggs, sausages, butter, and ham. People decorate eggs in brightly colored patterns. These eggs are called *pisanki*.

Did You Know?
Eggs are a symbol of life.

On Good Friday, women bake bread called *paska*. They may decorate paska with crosses, flowers, and birds made from dough.

On Easter Sunday, people enjoy a feast of the food that was blessed by the priest. The pisanki are cut into pieces and shared with wishes for good health and happiness. Easter Monday brings a tradition called Smigus-Dyngus. It is a fun-filled day when people drench each other with buckets and balloons full of water.

Polish teens take part in Smigus-Dyngus in Krakow. The water is a blessing of good fortune, or luck.

Constitution and Independence Day

Constitution Day celebrates the creation of Poland's constitution in 1791. Military parades and concerts take place across the country on May 3. People often gather at the Tomb of the Unknown Soldier in Warsaw. There, they honor all the unknown soldiers who have died defending Poland.

Poland's Flag Day is celebrated on May 2. Children in Krakow wave the Polish flag.

In 1918, at the end of World War I, Poland became **independent** after being ruled over by others for more than 125 years. Each November 11, the country celebrates its independence with church **masses** and parades. **Patriotic** songs and dances are also part of the celebration.

Parades are a big part of Independence Day festivities.

Krakowiak is a lively dance performed on special holidays by dancers in brightly colored traditional costumes.

Corpus Christi

Corpus Christi is a day of worship in Poland. It is one of the most important days on the calendar of the Catholic Church. The celebrations happen during May or June. On this day, people remember that Jesus Christ sacrificed his life for the world. In Poland, it is also known as Boze Cialo.

Priests lead the parades held in honor of Corpus Christi.

People take part in parades in towns and cities across Poland. They carry banners and pictures. The parade stops at four **altars** along the way, where people say prayers and sing hymns. Many houses and streets along the way are decorated with flowers, wreaths, and religious figures.

Parade participants sprinkle flowers in the streets to honor Jesus.

Did You Know? Corpus Christi is a Latin phrase which means "body of Christ."

St. John's Eve

St. John's Eve, on June 24, celebrates the birth of St. John the Baptist. It takes place around the summer solstice, which is the longest day of the year. It is also called Midsummer Night. It is a celebration of summer and the promise of young love. The evening ends with spectacular fireworks displays.

On St. John's Eve, people float candle-lit wreaths on the Vistula River (below).

Traditionally, large bonfires were lit in farmers' fields. People believed fire kept away bad luck. Girls wearing white clothing danced in circles around the bonfire, singing love songs. They made wreaths from herbs and flowers, called *wianki*. These were placed in a nearby river.

Did You Know?
In the past, girls believed that the boy who pulled her wreath from the river would one day become her husband.

Harvest Festival

Poland's Harvest Festival is celebrated at the end of the harvest in August. It is also called Dożynki. The farmers bring in the harvest during the last weeks of summer. They carry big bundles of herbs and vegetables to church. These are blessed by the priest.

In this small village, fruits, grains, and flowers are displayed at Harvest Festival.

After church mass, everyone enjoys a feast of the harvest's foods. This is followed by a celebration of singing and dancing. A harvest wreath called a Wieniec is woven of the most important grains of wheat and rye. It is decorated with flowers and ribbons and presented to the person who owns the fields. Traditional Polish costumes are often worn to celebrate this tradition.

Did You Know?
The Wieniec wreath is a symbol of a plentiful harvest.

Traditional costumes from different areas of Poland are brightly colored with detailed **embroidery**.

All Saints' Day

Every November 1, Polish people honor family members who have died. They believe that these people's souls can return to visit them on All Saints' Day. Many Polish families go to cemeteries where they place flowers, wreaths, and candles on the graves of their friends and family. On this day, the cemeteries are lively, happy, and colorful places!

Did You Know?
All Saints' Day is also known as the Day of the Dead.

Did You Know?
All Saints' Day, Wszystkich Swietych, is an ancient tradition that is more than 1,000 years old.

Families also prepare great feasts to welcome the souls for a meal. Extra places are set at the dinner table. Little fires are lit along the road to villages to show the souls their way home. Doors and windows are left open for the souls to easily enter and leave.

St. Andrew's Day

St. Andrew's Day is the name day of Saint Andrew. In Polish, it is called Andrzejki. St. Andrew's Day is held on November 30. Many years ago, it was believed that November 29 was a magical night when people could see into the future. To make predictions, they poured melted wax into a bowl of cold water. When it hardened, they looked at its shape to guess what might happen in the future.

Did You Know?
According to tradition, a girl tries to predict her husband by counting to the 14th post in a fence to see whether he will be large, thin, old, or young, just like the fence post.

Although people no longer believe they can see the future, they still like to pretend. Young women play games to predict whom they might marry. Young men join in the fun on November 25, the night of St. Catherine. That is when they have their fortunes told.

In Polish traditions, a young woman's future love was said to be revealed in her dreams on the night before St. Andrews's Day.

St. Barbara's Day

On December 4, people celebrate St. Barbara's Day. St. Barbara is the **patron saint** of coal miners in Poland. In Polish, it is called Barbórka. This is also known as Miner's Day. It is a day of festivals and celebrations to honor the men who work in Poland's mines. To celebrate, miners wear their traditional uniform of a black suit and hat with a feather.

Did You Know?
Poland is the one of the largest producers of coal in the world.

Once, there were more than 100 mines in Poland. The mines produced mostly coal, but also copper, silver, nickel, and salt. Mining was one of the most dangerous and honored professions in Poland. No mining work takes place on St. Barbara's Day.

The red, white, or black color of the feather on a miner's hat is a symbol of their status, or rank, among the workers.

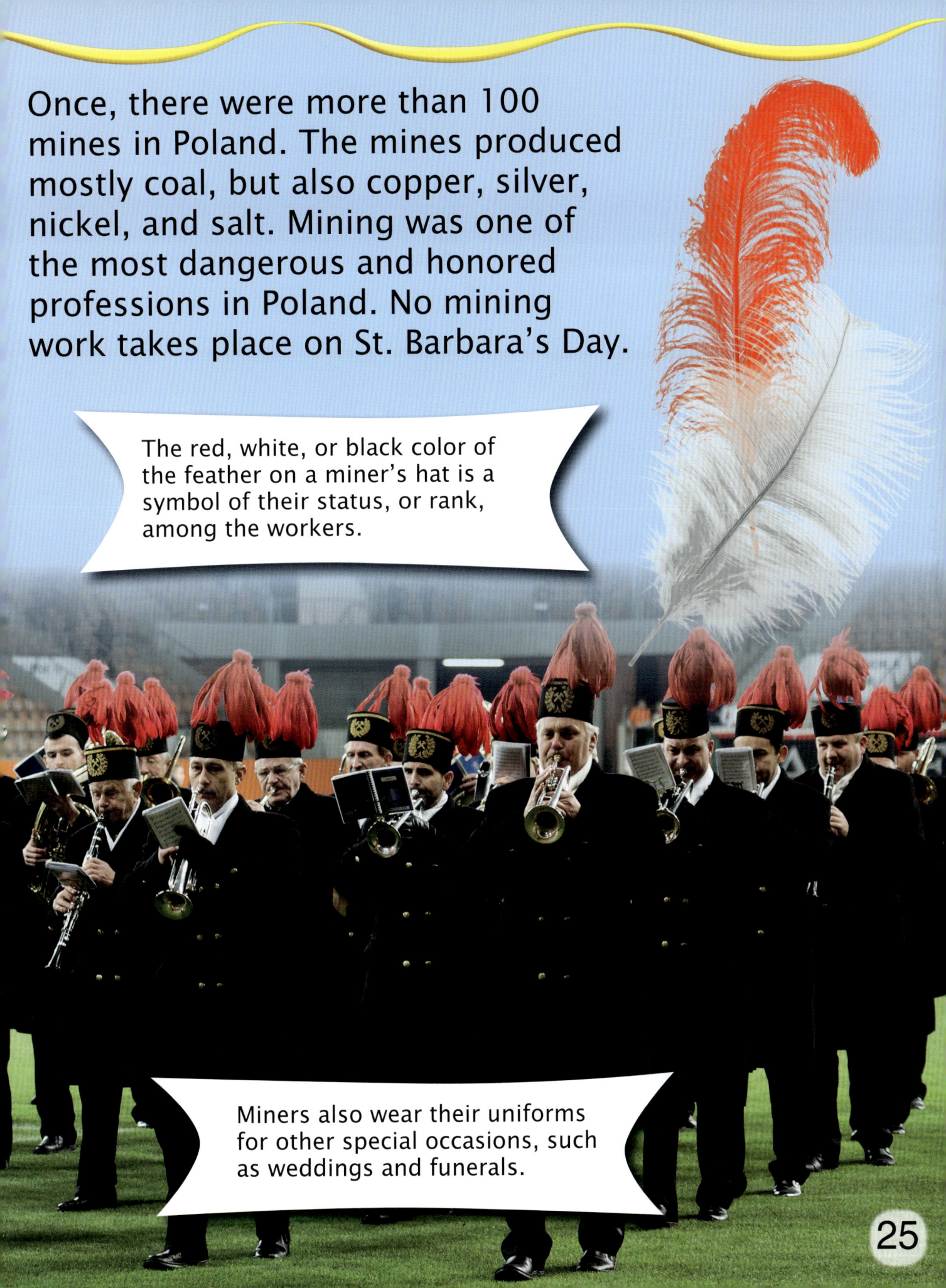

Miners also wear their uniforms for other special occasions, such as weddings and funerals.

Christmas Eve

Christmas is the most important holiday of the year. Celebrations take place over several weeks. St. Nicholas Day is on December 6. This is when St. Nicholas, or Swiety Mikolaj, visits children. He brings presents to those who have been nice, or a cane made of a birch tree branch for children who have been naughty.

Did You Know? It is traditional to put hay under the tablecloth to remember Jesus in his manger.

On Christmas Eve, families put up a Christmas tree. They decorate it with apples, oranges, small wrapped chocolates, nuts, and candles. The Christmas Eve feast begins when the first star, Gwiazdka, appears in the night sky. Family members break a thin wafer, or cracker, called *oplatek* and share good wishes for the year ahead. After dinner, many families attend a church mass called "Shepherd's Watch", or Pasterka.

A traditional Christmas Eve dinner includes mushroom soup, pickled herring, a type of fish, cheese- or potato-filled dumplings called perogies, stuffed cabbage rolls, and a cake called *babka*.

Did You Know?
An extra place is set at the dinner table for unexpected guests. In Polish culture, no one should spend Christmas alone.

Christmas Day

Christmas Day is on December 25. It is a day to relax, pray, and visit with family members. The day begins with a traditional breakfast of scrambled eggs, cold meats, smoked salmon, and pickled salads.

December 26 is St. Stephen's Day. It is the beginning of 12 nights of parades and caroling called Herody. Boys in special costumes perform scenes from the life of King Herod, who lived during Jesus' time. **Nativity scenes**, called *szopka*, are carried in the parades.

Did You Know?
Many of the szopka are inspired by the beautiful designs of Polish churches. They can be up to 6 feet (1.8m) high!

The Feast of the Epiphany, on January 6, ends the Christmas celebrations. Priests visit homes and write the initials of the three kings who visited Jesus' birth on or above the front doors. This is to protect the homes from bad luck.

Did You Know? The initials of the three kings are KMB. The kings were named Kaspar, Melchior, and Balthazar.

New Year's Celebrations

On New Year's Eve, Polish families celebrate the end of the year with bonfires and parties. Horse-pulled sleigh rides are popular in the countryside. People make wishes for health, happiness, and good fortune on New Year's Day. Bread shaped like a ring or cross is often hidden at the dinner table and used to tell each family member's fortunes.

People also bake bread in the shape of different animals, such as sheep, rabbits, and geese. They are given to children as blessings.

Old superstitions once suggested ways to bring good luck for the New Year. One claimed that to have good luck all year, you should only touch the floor with your right foot when getting out of bed.

Did You Know?
People also believed that to get rich in the New Year, you should put all your coins in a small purse. Then you run through the fields, shaking the bag and making noise.

Horse-pulled sleigh rides are a popular New Year's activity in Poland's countryside.

31

Glossary

altar A platform used for worship

constitution A system of principals and laws that define a country and its government

embroidery Stitches of thread that create patterns to decorate a piece of clothing

independent Free to rule itself

mass A Christian celebration

nativity scene The recreation of the scene which shows Jesus in his manger, his mother Mary, father Joseph, and the Three Kings

patriotic Showing strong support or love for your country

patron saint A person who is believed to protect a certain place or certain people

priest A religious or church leader who performs ceremonies such as marriages or funerals

Roman Catholic A large Christian church with 1.3 billion followers that is based in Rome, Italy. The Pope is its leader.

saint A holy person in the Catholic religion

Slavic A group of languages and people from central, eastern, and southern Europe

superstition Beliefs based on magic or legends instead of facts

Index

birthdays 6
Catholic celebrations 4, 6, 14-15, 26-29
coal miners 24-25
costumes 7, 13, 16, 17, 19, 28
dancing 13, 17, 19
Day of the Dead 20-21
Death Sunday 8
Dożynki 18-19
feasts 10, 21, 27, 29
foods 7, 10-11, 27, 28, 30
language 5
location of Poland 4
Midsummer Night 16-17
parades 12-13, 14-15, 28
pisanki 10-11
predicting the future 22-23
Smigus-Dyngus 11
Sto Lat 6
superstitions 8, 9, 31
Tomb of the Unknown Soldier 12
traditions 5, 8, 11, 13, 17, 20, 24, 28
wreaths 16, 17, 19, 20